Good to meet you!
Tim Weber
5/7/12

Gutters & Roses

Tim Weber

authorHOUSE®

AuthorHouse™
1663 Liberty Drive, Suite 200
Bloomington, IN 47403
www.authorhouse.com
Phone: 1-800-839-8640

First published by AuthorHouse 1/8/2009

ISBN: 978-1-4389-2779-4 (sc)

Printed in the United States of America
Bloomington, Indiana

This book is printed on acid-free paper.

"This is a true story of how God brought me from sleeping in gutters, under bridges, abandoned houses and drugs to a life filled with roses. It is a riveting story of the destruction that drug and alcohol addiction brings not only to addicts, but to those who love them."

Tim Weber

Psalms 40-2

"He lifted me out of the slimy pit, out of
the mud and mire; he set my feet on a rock
and gave me a firm place to stand"

Table of Contents

Foreward

Over the last 30 years I have personally seen how drugs have affected individuals, families, and communities. Working the streets as an undercover Maryland State Police Narcotics Officer and then as a Carroll County Drug Investigator; I have worked closely with the school system, juvenile services, drug treatment court, diversion programs, such as Choices, Community Conference, Heroin Action Coalition and other support groups. This is where the author and our paths crossed.

My first impression of Tim was of his sincerity of helping anyone involved with alcohol or drugs. He was a recovering addict with close to 5 years of clean time. He was literally on the street as a "junkie" but was able to rise above and mend his relationships with his family and be a successful member of society. He speaks of his life experiences in an attempt to keep other young people from walking in his shoes. His story is quite profound and will give the reader an eye opening picture of what it is like to be addicted to drugs. It also gives hope that it is possible to make changes and turn your life around; he is a walking testament to that. It took years of living on the street and several near death experiences; before he decides to do what he needs to do to break the chain of addiction.

This is a must read for anyone wanting to understand the tribulations of addiction. Whether you yourself are struggling, or are in recovery, or an enabler, a family member, or even a child of an addict; the author relates to all. This is a "G" rated version and suitable for all ages. Tim uses his candid recollection to depict what his life was like suffering from a drug addiction and ultimately how many people he affected. He is one of the lucky ones and has chosen to share his story to help others. You will find his honesty and insight insurmountable.

George A. Butler

Carroll County State's Attorney's Office

Drug Investigator

Introduction:

My hope is that this book will help others in the world suffering from the disease of addiction. I spent years upon years struggling with drugs and alcohol and finally was led out by the ever-loving grace of God and a twelve step recovery program. As you read through this book you will despise the person I became in my active addiction, and I hope that you see the depths we can go to as addicts. But there is a happy ending to this horrific story so I pray you will receive a message of hope and understand it is not the person you should despise, but the disease. I know God saved me so that I can tell this story to everyone. It took many years for the seed that was planted in me long ago to finally fertilize and grow. Now that it has, I hope and pray I can do the same, give a message of hope and plant the seed of God in someone so they will in return pass it on to others. I thank God for the message that Mickey at The Ranch gave me years ago. He was the very first person that introduced me to God and I will be forever indebted to him. It took years for that seed to grow, but it is growing daily, because of the message God allowed me to hear from him. The most important friend you will ever have is the person who introduces you to Jesus Christ!

Tim Weber

Poems I wrote while in Jail.

Under the Bridge

I used to drive over this bridge in my car;
God, if I had only known drugs would take me this far.

It was under this bridge that I drew blood red;
all the faces around me all looked dead.

An old woman sipping and nursing her wine,
how did you end up in this homeless shrine?

The smell and stench was more than I could bear,
if I could only get one more fix, I could mask my despair.

The night finally came and I was thrown in jail,
there I was all alone in my cell.

I dropped to my knees and cried to the Lord;
He answered me back and sent me a sword.

I read through the book and prayed once again,
just open your heart and let me back in!

Tim Weber

Lost in the Game

I was on my own and lost in the game; my life was filled
with sorrow and shame.

My biggest fear I had everyday was someone will find
me and take me away;

My biggest hope I had everyday is someone will find me
and take me away.

I lived on the streets with so much fear, but this is
something no one could hear.

I look at the people living there lives, going to work,
and hugging their wives.

God I wish I could get out of this game, and shed this
life of sorrow and shame!

I know there was a time when I could smile, but now
there is no way with all this denial.

The day finally came and had a touch from above; it was
sent to me in a message of love.

Now I am not on my own nor lost in the game because
I have been saved in Jesus' name!

Tim Weber

Part One

What it was like

The Mom I Barely Knew

It was December 6, 1976, about 8:30 in the morning. I was eleven at the time and most definitely a mama's boy. I walked into my room where my mother was sleeping. She had slept in my bed because my dad and she were fighting the night before. The night of the fight was just like many before; my dad was screaming and yelling at Mom, to this day I still don't know what it was about. I just know it happened a lot. Anyway, as I was going through my sock drawer I noticed my brother Pat sitting on the bed next to my mom. He looked at me and said, "Mom's not breathing."

I stared at him in disbelief. He screamed, "Go get Dad!"

I ran to my dad's room and banged on the door and in a panic screamed, "Mom is dead!"

He flew out of the shower dripping wet and ran to my room and shook her and shook her! He then picked up the phone and called 911. "I need an ambulance, at…" I do remember that he could not even remember our address; he was most definitely in shock. The next few minutes I really don't remember, I just know I was told to leave the room and go to the living room; minutes later there was an ambulance at our door and EMTs rushing back to my room.

I must have been in a trance. I remember this part like it was yesterday. I sat in my dad's recliner with my dog Oreo. Dogs are smart and even he knew I needed him in my lap just looking up at me and licking my face; in his own way he was taking care of me. I just watched all the activity in my house. I do not remember shedding one tear at that time. We loaded up and went to the Picayune Memorial Hospital, as at the time we were living in Picayune, Mississippi. I remember sitting in the waiting room and wondering what in the world was going on. Then a grim-faced doctor came out and said, "She is gone, I am sorry, sir." I think he said she was dead on arrival.

I watched my Dad and Pat closely and don't really remember any of us crying. I could be wrong, but as I recall it that is the way it was. I guess we were all in shock.

My brother Mike was off at college so we had to drive to his school and break the news to him. I remember walking down the corridor to my brother's dorm room; I was a few steps behind Pat and, he behind Dad. All I remember was the look on Mike's face. He knew something was wrong, why else would we all be there in the middle of the week? I didn't hear what Dad said. I just saw Mike collapse in Dads' arms and start sobbing. That was the first I remember crying about my mom's death at all, it was like, ok, Mike is, so I can too. I don't know where that came from, but that was how I felt. Mike was my idol.

So we all got in the car and drove back home. I remember thinking all the way back home, what am I going to do? Just last night I took my mom a glass of water and she told me she loved me and I said I love you too. And now she is dead! How could this happen? I was eleven years old and just lost my one and only emotional caretaker, my mom! I was lost, scared and felt all alone. The funeral was at a big church. I don't recall the name. I remember my mom had really gotten into church months before she died. Looking back now it gives me a good feeling to know she was a Christian. I only recall three things about the funeral. There were a lot of people I did not know, my Dad had one tear roll down his face and was gritting his teeth as to hold back any emotion. It was never verbally told to me but this is when I must have learned to show no emotion (unless of course it was rage, which I learned very well). It was basically not allowed in my family. Lastly, my dad set me, Pat and Mike on the bed at our house after the funeral and said, "Well, boys, it is just going to be us from now on."

The Dad I Feared

Now I must go back to the few years I had with my mom and dad together. Let's just say it was not too good from what I remember. I was very young and I know my mom was sick with arthritis. My dad was a very scary man as I recall it. I remember countless nights of screaming and yelling coming from the living room and I would cower down in-between my two brothers shaking and crying. My oldest brother Mike would always comfort me and say everything would be ok. But as a scared little boy all I knew was my mom was in trouble out in the other room. And when was it going to start on one of us!

My dad was an excellent provider and took very good care of us financially. So this part of my story is hard to write for the fear of the hurt it could cause him. However, I feel it needs to be told to get the true understanding of what my life was like through my eyes as a child. I love him dearly and our relationship today is one that includes friendship and a normal father son relationship, which I will get into in the later chapters.

So here goes. Point blank I was scared to death of my dad. I watched him beat my brother for using drugs. The night it happened I remember sitting on our couch in Houston watching television when Mike came in from somewhere. He sat down for a minute or two. He was drinking a Dr. Pepper (he was always drinking Dr. Pepper). He then said good night to us all and went back to his room. Well, minutes later my dad followed him and minutes after that he called me, Mom and Pat to come watch him beat the living heck out of Mike. And he looked at us and said, "This is what is going to happen to any of you who use drugs! "I remember my mom trying to jump on him and stop him but he just pushed her away. I can't tell you what was going on in my mind at that time, but even as I write it now I can see it in color! I was probably six or seven at the time.

There was another time when my brother Pat was caught smoking and my dad made him eat a whole pack of cigarettes! The sad thing is they weren't Pat's, they belonged to neighbor friends. Pat did smoke, but these just weren't his. And then we all went out to eat at a pizza place right after that like nothing happened.

My dad demanded respect! It was a must in our house to say "yes sir" or "no sir." And trust me you did not want to lie to him or even come close to disrespecting him. One time I had some friends over, from next door and we were playing late one night and probably being too loud in the living room and my dad was in one of those moods. Well, he came out and ripped me up by my underwear and it scared me so much I wet myself. I was maybe five or six years old and I still remember that night. I can't tell you the embarrassment I felt in front of those two friends.

I can say this: my father loves his three boys. And he did the best he could do. After the death of my mom things got better. He was still tough and led the house with an iron fist. But he was, I am sure, scared and wondering how in the world he was going to raise three boys on his own. But he did the best he could at the time and times were different back then. He thought if we feared him we would respect him and do well. And he has all the respect in the world from me! He has taught me some of my most valuable assets today, honesty and one heck of a work ethic. I don't think I have ever heard my father tell a lie.

You're Not My Mom!

Not too long after Mom died Arlene came into my life. She was my dad's girlfriend and let me tell you she paid for it. I was the youngest of the three boys and I gave her the most grief. She was not my mom and I let her know every day that she was no part of our family. After all, six months earlier my dad told me it was going to be just us four now. And that didn't include some woman trying to interfere with that. She did not want to take the place of my mom, but being dad's girlfriend and eventually moving in with us she had no choice. Whether she wanted it or not, in my eyes she was an evil step-mother! I hated her with a passion.

Here it is almost three decades later and I could not be more proud to call Arlene my mom. How this woman stuck it out with my dad and the three of us and our addictions still amazes me. She is one of the most precious people in my life today. And I love her dearly and value her not only as a mother but as a very good friend.

The Addiction Begins

This is where my story leads to a point in my life where I learned to not feel and to stuff every emotion humanly possible.

I can tell you I don't remember my first drink, but I remember my first drunk like it was yesterday.

I know there were times before eight years old when I had snuck sips of beer and wine at family functions or my father's company picnics. But it meant nothing, because I never drank enough to feel any affects of the alcohol. But that all changed the summer before the ninth grade when I was invited to a party with some older kids who were already in high school. Well, they had a lot of beer and weed. I don't remember smoking any weed, but I sure remember the beer. And I thought I had found the answer I had been looking for all of my short life. It made me everything I thought I wanted to be, and most importantly everything I thought everyone else wanted me to be. I was no longer shy, timid, and afraid and I flat out thought I could do anything that night. I was accepted into a new class of people, the older cool people. Little did I know that first feeling of being drunk would eventually lead me down a road of destruction to living under bridges and abandoned houses.

I remember waking up the next morning and my head was spinning I threw up, and felt like my head had been hit by a Mack truck. However; I could not wait to do it again as soon as possible! And I did it many times after that with the same effect of pleasure and then pain. This continued all summer long and then school started and I attended my first High School, Wilde Lake High School. I was playing football and meeting new people and life was good. So I thought. One day a guy was in school and had some Quaaludes, I think his dad was a doctor or something. Well, I bought a couple and instead of waiting till after school I took mine right away.

Thirty minutes later I was out of control. I couldn't walk, and needless to say I found myself in the office and waiting for someone to pick me up. I don't remember much about the ride home but I do remember waking up and my dad standing over me. As you can imagine I was pretty scared of what he was going to do. Well, there was no butt kicking. It was worse. He looked me square in the eyes and said, "Don't you know that is how your mother died, from an overdose of pills?"

This sent me into a whirlwind of emotions from that point on about everything. I convinced myself that Mom had killed herself because she couldn't take my dad or us three boys anymore. Years later he told me it was congestive heart failure. So here I am thirteen already suspended from school and we hadn't even had our first football game. And it does not end there with Wilde Lake High. Two weeks after returning to school someone had some purple micro dots (LSD) and once again I got some and couldn't wait until after school to do mine. We were having testing at school that day, the one where you fill in the multiple choice dots. The acid kicked in and I was once again out of control. I could not stop laughing in class so I was sent to the office. They could not tell what I had done because other than my pupils being quite dilated I seemed fine, just a little too happy. They sent me to the nurse's station to either wait for the police to come or my dad; to be honest, at that time I would have preferred it be the police!

About an hour went by and a couple of friends walked by the nurse's station and looked in on me when the nurse had walked out for a minute. They both said, "Dude, you better get out of here, just leave and tell them you don't know what was wrong with you and come back tomorrow."

I think they thought that if they found out I was on acid I would tell who I got it from or get in a lot of trouble. Probably tell. In any case, I scooted out of school unnoticed and walked around the lake for hours hoping the drugs would wear off and I could go home and no one would know. Wrong! I walked through the doors of my house and Dad and Arlene were sitting at the kitchen table waiting for me. But to my surprise I didn't get my head caved in. It was just a look of disappointment and shame. A look I grew to know very well in the years to come. We talked for hours and to be honest I don't know what was said. I was still tripping on the acid and their faces were melting right before my eyes. I am not trying to glamorize that in any way, it is just the truth.

The next day I got the news I was expelled from school and that meant no going back to Wilde Lake High School. Before I crawled out of bed that morning I was listening to 98 Rock and heard the breaking news: "John Lennon has been shot and killed outside his apartment." I don't know why I remember this, it is not like I was a big Beatles fan. I just remember the morning and thinking that news didn't seem nearly as bad as mine. I was already a self-centered addict.

The Move to Centennial High School

Somehow my dad got me enrolled in another high school. We happened to have just moved into another school district, Centennial High School. I was not happy about this to say the least. All my friends were at Wilde Lake and now I have to go to another school with this big stigma attached to me. I was the kid who flipped out on drugs at Wilde Lake. Well, it didn't take me long to get a new stigma at school: "The Boxer," the kid who would fight anyone.

When I was twelve years old my brother Mike took me to the movie "Rocky." I fell in love with boxing. I started in Slidell, Louisiana, where we moved a few months after my mom died. I started out at 95 pounds and was in a lot of fights in the Slidell and New Orleans area. When we moved to Maryland I had gotten out of it for a year or so until I found a boxing club in Catonsville. I had a few fights around here and a few write-ups in the paper and was known as Tim the Boxer, or Tex's little brother. That was my middle brother Pat's nickname since we were originally from Texas, where he was very well known for his fights in school and at parties around the area. The funny thing is we had this reputation and when people would see us they would say those are the tough guys, they can't weigh 140 pounds soaking wet!

OK, back to school. I guess I am saying I could use my fists very well and was always more than a little eager to show this skill off at school. I was in school for maybe one week and someone said something to me they shouldn't have. So out the wood shop door we went and I unloaded some combinations on him and he bled severely from the nose. I found out later he was a diabetic and bled easily. Believe it or not I felt bad about this for many years. But hey, he started it and he raised his hands and to me that meant hit or be hit. Anyway, it was the talk of the school and there you go. I had a new reputation I was proud of. All the time deep down inside I was scared of my own shadow. I just figured if I could take a punch from my dad and not fight back, if I can fight back no one could beat me up. Let me tell you, however, that I found out on a number of occasions that philosophy was off. I got my share of the worst in many fights through the years.

Well, the very next day the administrator of the school got wind of this and there I was in an office in trouble again. Thank God this man had us shake hands and promise not to take it any further. I agreed and I thought that was that. Then he asked the other kid to go back to class and he wanted to talk to me alone. These are the words I remember.

"I understand you are a pretty good boxer, so let me ask you this: why did you feel the need to beat the heck out of someone who couldn't fight their way out of a wet paper bag?"

In my defense at this time I was fighting in the 139 pound weight class and was maybe 5'8", this guy was at least 6', ok, maybe he was skinny but he ran his mouth to the wrong new kid. I didn't say all that but I was thinking it.

21

"Mr. Weber, here is your warning. You get in another fight, you will be expelled from my school too. I don't care if someone calls you every name in the book, or raises their hand to you. You come to me and I will deal with it."

The funny thing is this man and I became close I had a couple of situations come up that year and I actually went to him and told him, no names of course, but I at least got it out there. He always followed my fights and was supposed to come to a couple of them but never made it to any. I found out just recently from someone I met through my business that he passed away a few years ago.

So life went on at Centennial. I met and got close to many people. A few I have to mention are Toby, Rick, Kurt and James. We did everything together. Toby and I were the closest. He actually went to Atholton High School and was a state champion golfer, I think two years in a row. Man, I loved Toby! The reason I say loved in the past tense is because he died of this disease several years ago. I was devastated but I was already so far gone in my own addiction I couldn't even make it to his funeral. I will get to that later. Let me just say when you saw Toby you saw me, and vice versa, always. He lived with me for a while during high school. God, do I miss him; I know he would be so proud of me for being clean! Anyway, we all had fake ID's and let me tell you we did all our college partying in high school. Coast to Coast, drink and drown night every Thursday from 11th grade all the way through the 12th. We would always have a bong, bag of weed and brews every weekend and throughout the week. We always partied.

My Dreams and Aspirations Destroyed

The one thing that half way saved me from becoming a worse drug addict through high school was boxing. From the time I saw Rocky, I knew what I wanted to be when I got older and I was well on my way. I was going to go to the Olympics, then become the middle weight champion of the world. I had my Lamborghini picked out, my house and that was that. You could not tell me any different. It was a dream that I really let nothing interfere with, not girls, not alcohol, not drugs. What I mean is when I had a fight coming up I would put it all down and train, make weight, fight and then party.

That all changed in 1982. I was up for the title fight and had I won this fight I surely would have had a shot at the Olympic trials. Well, I have to tell you leading up to this fight there was a lot of hoopla. I had won a fight a month before where I had to lose a lot of weight in two weeks. There was a big write-up in the paper and I was ready. Sugar Ray was fighting Roberto Duran, not on my card (of course), just that was the era. Fighting was a big thing. And for me it was everything. The stands were packed. I had friends, family and my girlfriend all there in anticipation.

But the night started off bad. I was overweight hours before the fight, so they gave me a chance to lose it prior to the final weigh in. It was only maybe a half-pound or so and you can sweat and spit that off quickly. And I did. I got in the ring and the crowd was screaming, The very first round I got my bell rung good. I didn't go down but

I was seeing double for sure. I made it to the middle of the 3rdround (amateur fights are three, two minute rounds) and they stopped it. TKO! I had never been stopped and it killed me. Don't get me wrong, this guy was good, and he had me from the first punch. All I could do was try shoving him to the ropes and swing, not my style. Up until then I won by boxing, moving and jabbing.

Mr. Summer, the father of one of my best friends, said to me, "Tim, you swung, he countered, and he rocked you every time." I was devastated after that. My life was over as I knew it. This was when my life took a major turn. I picked up a six pack of tall boys on the way home from that fight and never laced up another pair of gloves competitively.

I was seventeen when my short boxing career ended and I had one more year of high school left. Most of my close friends were a year older and already off to college. I had other friends but Toby was gone to school on a golf scholarship and I was stuck here in high school to fend for myself. I was still playing lacrosse and I was a starting crease attack man that year. The drinking and pot use increased to daily and heavy. I could always play lacrosse even after an all night bender.

It was the day before one of our County rival games and I got in another fight in school and I was not suspended but I was not allowed to play in that game. I will never forget my coach saying to me, "I never thought there would come a day when I would be saying to you. I was depending on you and need you for this game and you screwed it up." Man that felt good and hurt all at the same time. But once again I saw that look of disappointment. In any case, graduation came and I graduated, somehow, and my high school years were now behind me.

DWI

I was now out of high school and had really no plans. I couldn't go to any four year schools because my grades were too bad. So we found a junior college in Texas for me to go to. I was excited about it, it had dorms and a friend of mine from school was going with me. It was in a sense a new start. Well, the summer before we left I had my first encounter with the law. I was driving home from a bar in Catonsville, Maryland. I was drunk, bad drunk as I recall, and I was throwing up out of my truck. I saw lights, red and blue and that was that, I had a DWI at 18. The thing was the cop gave me a ride home and I was off to Texas and school before my dad knew anything. Trust me that would not happen today, that was in 1983. I got a slap on the wrist and one year of probation and I was on my way.

My College Career

It was two weeks before school started and my dad, a friend I graduated high school with and I were on our way to Texas. It is about a 24 hour drive to Texas from Maryland and we could not wait to get there. At this time my dad had a farm in Texas. We had land and a cabin. I never figured out why we always called it a farm. Anyway, we went to the campus first, Henderson County Junior college in Athens, Texas. Then we went to the farm where we picked up a quarter pound of weed from an old babysitter of mine and her husband. He was a truck driver and probably one of the craziest people I had met up until this point in my life. We spent a few days at the farm and then off to school. So there we were. We had weed so we were immediately accepted by the partiers and the party was on. I started classes and all was going well. I was now free and away from the father I feared, able to stay out all night, drink and get high with no fear of repercussions from my dad. Somehow I made it through the first semester of school ok. I had a 3.0 grade point average and was actually going to class.

All that changed one night when we all went to a club in Tyler, Texas. Our school was in a dry county in Texas so you had to go to another town to go clubbing. I don't remember the name of the club, but I do remember that I was introduced to "Crystal Meth," a drug I had never even heard of prior to this night. I tried it. Why not, everyone else was doing it, so how bad could it be? I snorted one line and I was up (wired to the gills) for fourteen hours at least! I talked, I talked, and did I say I talked and I mean non stop you could not shut me up. I was going up to people I had never met and by the end of the night I was best friends with everyone in that bar. So just like that first buzz at thriteen and I had found the answer, now I had truly found the answer. It wasn't even three days later. I was looking for the guy we got it from and found him and he invited my roommate and I out to his trailer and I got it again. This is the point where EVERYTHING was about to change for the worse.

The Needle and the Spoon

There were people there injecting this drug into their arms with hypodermic needles. Needless to say I said, "I want to try that." No questions asked; they showed me how. It was drawn up in a spoon and one of the guys there put a belt around my arm and told me to look away. Then there was a little pinprick and BOOM it hit me and now I had truly found what I had been looking for! It was instant. I was hooked and I was hooked on the needle. I learned that night just about anything can be broken down with a little water and drawn into a syringe and injected. From that day forward I never snorted anything ever again. I would have shot up a birth control pill if I thought it might get me high. My addiction was brewing up in me like a hurricane building strength and steam at sea. Just looking for a place to land, which would later come to be anyone close to me. My dad, my brothers, Arlene, girlfriends, and my children - it did not matter. From this point on it went quickly from a Category One and eventually to a Category Five at the end! I had a checking account connected to my dad's in Maryland at the time and I started slowly writing checks for this drug and eventually started not going to class at all and soon enough there was no more school.

Fatherhood Begins

It was sometime in the fall of 1984. I was outside my dorm with some friends and a van drove by. It was a carload of girls. I don't remember all their names but one of them became the mother of my children. They stopped and told us that there was a party that night at one of their houses; they were local girls in the town, not students at the college. Well, one of the girls was obviously interested in me and I must say I was interested in her. She was a beautiful little Southern girl. We didn't even really get a chance to go on a date other than that first night at the party and I was being kicked out of school. The dean of the school called me into his office, once again even in college, I am being called into an office. I was in trouble! He said, "Mr. Weber, you can't stay on campus anymore, this is not an apartment and you have no classes, so therefore I must ask you to leave."

I was devastated, but not because I had probably blown my education. No, I might have to move back to Maryland with my dad. This is when I started to become a con and a manipulator. I was able to convince my new girlfriend of two weeks that I was going to have to move back to Maryland if I didn't find a place to stay. I told her I just had dropped a class or two and was below a fulltime student load and had to stay somewhere for the semester till next semester. So she went to her parents and they agreed to let me stay with them. The truth of the matter is I was out of school completely. I will admit I was smitten by the girl; however, the thought of moving back home was out of the question. At the time all this was going down my father was out of the country on business. So when he returned I was able to fill him in and make him think everything was ok. I would stay with my girlfriend and her family, and get back to a full load the next semester.

But that's not what happened. I was using crystal meth as much as possible and getting worse day by day. My girlfriend had no idea, her family had no idea. The only people who knew were my friend I had come to school with, the guy I got the meth from and a few other guys at school.

Megan & Michael

About two weeks after I moved in with my girlfriend she was pregnant and Megan was on the way. I was getting so far gone by that point, that it was sad. There was no way I was capable of love, I couldn't love anyone, including myself. So here I am, nineteen, no job, out of school, and let's not forget the hurricane of addiction that is growing daily! We now had to get married (so I thought) and nine months later on September 10, 1985, Megan Ann came into this world.

Now what? I have this beautiful girl that I have to take care of. I wanted to, I just didn't know how. I didn't even know what an electric bill was. Let alone car payments, insurance, and all the bills that come with being an adult. She was the most beautiful thing I had ever seen. I must say after seeing, touching and holding my little girl I thought, ok, it is time for me to quit using drugs. How blessed I was to have a healthy child and it is time for me to grow up. However, as anyone who has experienced the power of addiction knows, those were just words.

It was not long after having Megan I was back to using as much as possible. I tried to only drink beer, but every time I would get drunk, I couldn't control myself and I was off looking for a shot of meth. Once I would do one shot I would disappear for days. And to say the least it just kept getting worse. On February 23, 1987, my son Michael Dale was born. Again he was the apple of my eye, a son to carry on the family name. Well, by this point I was most definitely at a Category Three in my addiction. I was starting to write hot checks, stealing from my wife's parents' flower business, and every word out of my mouth was a lie.

The Flower Business

My father-in-law owned a couple of flower shops at the time and through me not working a steady job, I could always go up there and deliver, clean, and really just steal, if I am being honest. After all, if I was up there working at least they weren't just giving me money to support my kids, and let's not forget the bad drug habit I had. I will say this, through my time in the flower shop I did learn to design flowers and this as you will see, came in handy through the years and now provides myself and family a good living. I know my father-in -law knew I was stealing and just didn't have the heart to say anything. He was one of the kindest, most honorable men I have ever known. It got to the point where every day he had to cash checks to put cash in the drawer to operate. Eventually he just basically gave my wife and me the shop. We started operating it and I really got to know the flower business. I was trying so hard to be a father, business owner, and husband, but I just could not fight of the demon of addiction. I would do ok for a week or two, and then I was off and running spending all our money and writing hot checks. I would say that in maybe one year I shot that whole flower shop up my arm!

The First of Many Rehabs

I must have been about twenty-one years old when I entered my first drug and alcohol rehab. I had no idea what to expect. I just knew this would get everyone off my back. I checked in and started my first shot at recovery. At this point I was someone who needed recovery, but by no means wanted it. As you will see later, in order to get recovery, that need most definitely has to turn into a want. This is where I was introduced to the twelve step program that would eventually introduce me to God, and save my life! I remember my first meeting was in the cafeteria in the rehab. I sat way in the back and a group of guys were already there up in the front. I think there were three of them, one guy read a bunch of stuff, the other guy just sat there, and then one of them spoke after all the readings, which were quite boring.

The guy who spoke was named Scott. He had long blonde hair and tattoos and looked to be about six feet tall. His face looked very rough like he had a hard life. He stood up and said, "My name is Scott and I am an alcoholic and drug addict, and thanks to God and the twelve steps I did not have to stick a needle in my arm, or take a drink of alcohol today." This caught my attention, so I perked up and listened. I don't remember all that was said that night but I do remember him saying that because of his addiction he went to prison for fifteen years. And since getting out he had attended twelve step meetings on a regular basis and does not ever turn down an opportunity to share his story with others. He said that for him it took going to prison but it does not have to be that way. You can stop now and get into recovery and have a good life. I felt like he was talking to me I know now it was most definitely God speaking through this man and planting a seed that would later grow and send me on a mission to help others with this deadly disease.

I wish I could say that was the only rehab I needed, but that is just not the way it was. I would eventually go through around eighteen rehabs, some lasting three days and a couple I went to for a year, one for eighteen months, and another couple for six months. So for me to go into each one of those rehabs would be impossible, so I will touch on a few throughout this part of the book. I remember getting out of that first rehab and going to my first twelve step meeting on my own. I was thinking, there is no way I can spend the rest of my life going to these meetings. Everyone in there was over forty and looked to be very boring. So I didn't go much more.

Instead I continued to use and use whatever I could. Crack had just started getting popular then and of course I tried it and liked it, so I now had another weapon in my arsenal to feed my addiction. I didn't really like it a lot but if I couldn't find any Meth I could always find crack, 24/7. This is the part where everything really got bad. I was doing whatever I had to do to get high. Mostly taking every penny I could from my wife, her family, and even stealing money out of my own kid's piggy bank. Finally my wife had enough and kicked me out and I moved to Houston to live with my older brother Mike who was going through a divorce at the same time. My dad had a house there he'd bought as an investment and Mike had been fixing it up for him. So he thought it would be a good Idea to let me go there and we could lean on each other. Well, we leaned all right. It was two hurricanes of addiction coming together to make "The Perfect Storm." This is where I would delve into a drug that would take every ounce of life out of me. Heroin! It robbed me of years upon years of freedom, life and almost took my breath (killed me) many times.

Heroin

I was twenty five years old when I took my first shot of black tar heroin. I was with my brother and some other guys in Houston. We drove to a house in a rough section of the city near the Astrodome. We walked into a house with a mom, a dad, and yes kids all around. The guy took us to a table in the kitchen and we all bought a twenty-five-dollar foil of tar. Being my first time with heroin I had someone break it down for me and draw it in the syringe and then I took over from there. I had been sticking needles in my arm for years now so I could do that. I do remember being scared so I put the needle in and only shot half of it in. BAM!!! It hit me and NOW THAT IS WHAT I HAVE BEEN LOOKING FOR! It gives you a feeling of euphoria that is out of this world. I did not care about anything, no kids, and no ex, nothing. I was to the point of comfortably numb. This is where I stayed for the next twelve years. Numb! One of the many bad things about this drug is, it wears off and you get physically hooked quickly. This is where everything gets foggy, so I will do my best to tell this part as I remember it.

I was hooked on heroin from the very first shot. I started out with doing just heroin, but soon, very soon started to speedball my stuff. That is when you mix heroin with cocaine and inject it. It is the same concoction that has killed a lot of famous people you have heard of. This is where that little boy from the past was buried; I was now a full blown addict. I had crossed a line where turning back was going to take a miracle, an intervention from God.

My brother and I were living in the house in Houston, supposedly fixing it up. We had bought a shower and tub insert from a store to put in the house. Well, it was about two hundred dollars so anytime we ran short on money we would return it to get the money and buy heroin. We did this at least three times, buy it, return it, buy it, and return it. Finally, one time we actually installed it so we couldn't very well return it again. Of course all this was done on my dad's money, he had an account set up for us so we could buy supplies for the house and for us to live. He was out of the country and had no idea what was going on. This is when I first learned a very valuable asset I had at this time. I say asset in jest, it was the time in my life when I became a master manipulator. I met a girl in Houston who was a single mother and went out on a date with her. Why she went I have no idea, but the next two days I conned her into letting me move in with her. I took money, food and anything she had over the small amount of time I spent with her. I even took money out of her account where she couldn't pay her rent. She came over to our house after I figured I had used her all I could, and tried to wake me up. I was high and not in the mood to listen to this girl gripe at me. I remember her saying, "How could you do this to me and my daughter? I had to go to my mother's and borrow money so I could feed my daughter." The fact is I did not care; heck, at this point I didn't care about anyone but myself and feeding my addiction. I was cold as ice, no emotion, and no feelings whatsoever.

This went on in Houston a while longer and my dad returned to the U.S. and we were about to be found out. My brother Pat was living in Maryland at the time and he was in a twelve step recovery program, and doing well. They got wind somehow of what was going on in Texas and both flew down to Texas for an intervention. Within hours I was on a plane on my way to Maryland to go into yet another rehab. My brother Mike was to stay back and help my dad close the house up. So I got the better end of that deal and was in rehab with medication to detoxify of my heroin addiction and Mike had to kick his habit in the car with my father all the way from Texas to Maryland, a twenty four hour drive straight through. I got to Maryland and checked into rehab and kicked heroin for the first time. Let me paint a picture for you of coming off a heroin addiction. It feels like the worst flu you have ever imagined, your bones ache to the core, your nose runs non-stop, you have uncontrollable diarrhea and your stomach aches with cramps. You are cold and chilled one minute, and hot the next and the depression makes you want to die! And this was in rehab, so I know my brother was really going through it worse. The one thing about heroin withdrawal is, it won't kill; you just want to kill yourself. If you do heroin for three days in a row you are going to go through some kind of withdrawal.

Well, I got out of rehab and was now living in Maryland. An old high school friend came to see me at the rehab and offered me a job when I got out. I probably hadn't been to Maryland in years so it was nice to have a change and I felt good and healthy after rehab. My brothers were both here and we saw each other a lot and even went to meetings together. So here I am living back in Maryland and working for my friend and all is well. But, recovery was not first, and God was nowhere in the picture so it wasn't long and I thought, well, maybe I can just drink beer. Wrong!

I was working for my friend at the deli and decided to start making some extra money by selling candy arrangements. It was an idea I picked up working for a company in Houston during the beginning stages of my heroin addiction. I worked for the company maybe two weeks. At the time I was already hooked on heroin and ended up stealing all the money out of the register and never came back. Having floral experience from my work at my ex-father-in-law's shop, it was very easy to pick this craft up. A candy arrangement is a bouquet made out of candy. They are really cool looking. So I started making them around Christmas time and selling them at the deli and it was not long before I was getting many orders. So being the entrepreneur I was, I was ready to quit the deli and go out on my own. I really always have had that entrepreneurial spirit in me – it's just the spirit of addiction would always win. I talked to my friend and he was behind me and in fact he wanted in on it and he put up the money to get started. We found a spot in the mall in Columbia, Maryland, actually a kiosk, so we were in business.

All was starting off good and we were selling bouquets and having fun. I had my friend Toby as a sales manager and he was getting hospital accounts and we were on our way. Just one big problem was about to interfere: me and my addiction. I had started drinking and Toby and I were having fun almost like we were in high school again. One night we were out at a bar and I got drunk and left the bar and went into Baltimore and found some heroin. Let me just say one thing I know for sure, if you're an addict and an alcoholic you can not try to substitute one for the other. Meaning, if you are a crack addict and you drink again you are going to go back to using crack. And if you are a heroin addict you are going to use heroin again. I put this to the test for many years and whether it was the first night I drank or two months later I always went back to heroin, always. So that night I went to the worst part of Baltimore I could find, drove by a corner, saw what I thought (no, I knew) were dealers and asked if they knew where I could get some boy. Boy is a street name for heroin in Texas, but obviously it was not called that here. They looked at me like I was crazy, so I rephrased it and found out in Baltimore it is called dope. And they even give the dope a name, like suicide, Bin Laden, killa, etc. Well, needless to say I picked up the lingo quickly. One name that is the same everywhere is" girl," that is cocaine. So I got a couple of pills of dope and two caps of girl and I was off and running again. I was able to hide this part of my addiction for a little while and just let a few people know that I was drinking. The friend I was partners with at the candy business was very upset and he had good reason. I was about to lose all his money he had invested.

Kentucky

It was not long after we opened our business that I ran into an old girlfriend from high school and started seeing her. The thing was she knew me very well and she had heard about my stints in rehab and was well aware of the fact that I was an alcoholic and addict. So while she was in town for a while with her daughter Polly, Mary and I started a fast and furious relationship. We had dated in high school and to my surprise I discovered that she had been in love with me since high school. So here it is almost ten years after high school and we both were parents and back together. After spending those few days together we really wanted it to go further. All the time I was hiding the fact that I was drinking and drugging again. After about a week or two of her going back home to Kentucky, she asked me to come to see her, or I asked her if I could come see her, I am not really sure who asked whom. In any case, I went to see her and that visit changed her and Polly's life for a long time. I went back to Maryland after a few days and we talked on the phone every day. I was now most definitely at a Category Four of my addiction and about to hit Kentucky, Mary and Polly. I had an old car; I think it was a 78 Ford Fairmont, so we talked about trying to have a long distance relationship. The problem was my old car barely got me to and from the mall, so there was no way it would go back and forth to Kentucky. She had an extra car she didn't use, a Porsche, to boot, that she said I could fly up and drive home to Maryland so I could work the business and drive to see her as often as I could. We went along for a little while with me driving back and forth from Maryland to Kentucky. I was drinking again pretty heavily, and driving to Baltimore and doing heroin all in Mary's car.

Well, things started really heating up between us and things were not going too good at the business since I was back on drugs and not only spending all the money, I wasn't even showing up at work. So one day I was on the phone with Mary crying the blues and missing her and her, me. "Just move here", she said.

"Ok," I said.

The next day I went to the mall before it opened and cleared out my cart and I think I even threw a lot of the stuff in the dumpster and headed for Kentucky. This caused me and one of my best friends to go our separate ways in anger. He was angry and rightly so, it was all his money that was going down the drain. And I know now he always knew I was a messed up addict and about to ruin Mary's life. He was right. I tried for many years to repair this relationship with him; the fact is I always tried when I wasn't serious about recovery. I hope one day to make amends with him. We probably won't ever be as good of friends as we were years ago, but I would still like to look him in the eyes and apologize, and for him to know that I mean it.

If Mary only knew the nightmare I was about to put her and Polly through. I moved in and I just kept getting worse. Mary owned a horse farm in Kentucky and was raising race horses. I must be honest, it was quite overwhelming, the place was unbelievable. Here I am trying once again to stay clean and start a new life. The one thing about the disease of addiction is that if not treated it just lays dormant, waiting for the right opportunity to rear its ugly head. And I was just trying to not use.

Things were great at first, but they went bad quickly. I was living with a woman who was a successful business woman in her field and the best I could do was make seven dollars an hour at a plant in Lexington, Kentucky. I just did not feel good about myself, and what I do when I feel bad is use drugs. And for the moment I would not feel better, but at least I was high and didn't feel. This was much better than the way I felt. It was not long before I started taking money from her credit cards and any loose money she would leave around the house. It was around Easter that year and some of her family was coming in for the holiday and I left that Friday to supposedly look for a job. I was really out smoking crack, I had even drove up to the farm late one night that weekend and sneaked into the barn where she kept the horse tranquilizers. I riffled through the small refrigerator and found some "ace" which I had watched her for months shoot in the vein of the neck of big race horses to tranquilize them to get them on a trailer. I had been smoking crack only because I couldn't find heroin, so I needed something to slow me down and I thought if this stuff knocks a horse out, maybe a small amount will make me feel just right. I even remember her asking me time and time again "does this bother you" when she was injecting a horse. I would always reply, "No, I am done with that life." As you will see, I was not done for many years.

I got the ace out of the fridge, found a horse needle that probably had a point on it the size of a match-stick, drew up a small amount, dropped my pants and jabbed the needle in my rear end. I was too scared to stick it in my vein, so a muscle shot would have to do. I put it all up, walked out of the barn and collapsed, looking up at the stars wondering if I had made a mistake. The fact is years later when Mary found out I had done this she told me if I had picked the other tranquilizer, I am not sure of the name; it would have killed me on the spot!

As it turned out, I woke up before dawn and drove off to spend another day of smoking crack. I often wondered how I drove up to the barn with the whole family there and no one knew. I stayed away till late Sunday night so I would show up after they had already left. Or so I thought. Her mom was still there and when I walked in I was surprised to say the least. Mary looked at me with the most disappointed, ashamed, and embarrassed look, that look I was starting to grow accustomed to. She said, "You are going to have to leave." I knew that was coming and was prepared for it. But I was not expecting to be on an airplane back to Maryland with her mom. Mary had told me before I left that if I asked her mom she would get me into "Father Martin's Ashley," a rehab in Maryland. Her family were big contributors to Father Martin's.

I waited till I got on the ground in Baltimore before I popped the question. We didn't sit together on the plane, and I honestly was glad because I was extremely ashamed. I walked up to her and asked her, "Would you please help me get into rehab?"

She looked at me and said, "You come out to my house tomorrow and I will talk to you about it."

I drove out the next day and that next day I was in rehab. I might as well say right here, it didn't stick. I went through thirty days of rehab on someone else's money and was out using soon after I got out of rehab. I was back using and eventually left Baltimore and moved back to Texas.

Texas Tornado

OK, so I had now burned my bridges in Maryland and Kentucky. So I thought I will go back to Texas and move to Dallas. I would be closer to my kids and a new start and I had been away long enough that it felt new. My Dad once again being the enabler father he was, he hooked me up with a car and an apartment in Big "D" (Dallas). I called my kids Megan and Michael, they were probably nine and eleven years old by now. I had seen them off and on through the last couple of years and talked to them as often as I could, when I was not getting high somewhere. My dad would always pay for them to come up to Maryland to see me.

So I had a nice apartment and was back on track again for a month or so. I got a job in the floral department of a big superstore chain. Once again that floral background came in handy. I was hired on the spot, and met many new friends and was doing ok. I kept it a secret that I was an addict and alcoholic and went out drinking with people from work. After all, I was in a new place and maybe this time I could handle it. Like I said before, if you are an alcoholic, you are an addict as well. You will always go back to your drug of choice. Some people may not agree with this but they are either not alcoholic, are they just haven't experienced it yet. There is a difference between someone who just drinks too much and an alcoholic; it is the phenomenon of craving, the obsession once started that can't be stopped without some interruption. For me the interruption came in the form of rehabs that you have already seen: jails and mental institutions.

The Original Candy Arrangement

I had been working at the store for maybe two months and was actually thinking; maybe I have this drinking under control. I am working and going out and having a few beers like all my normal friends. So no drugs - YET! I talked the people I worked for into letting me sell some of my candy arrangements through the store and while they did not do well there, they did get noticed. A manager from a large grocery store chain saw them and called me and said, "You have to take samples of these to my corporate office, I love them and want them in my store." I called the corporate office, and the receptionist said, "You have to send a brochure in and we will contact you if we think we can sell it."

In other words she was blowing me off. I said, "Miss, I don't have a brochure, can I come by and drop of a couple of samples?"

"Sure," she said, and she gave me the address and the next day I was there and dropped off a couple and the rest is history. They loved them, I got a call and they wanted to set up an appointment to meet me and my partner.

My business partner was once again a victim of my disease. Her name was Julie, and she worked at the same place I did and we made eye contact one day and that was that. I found out she was married so I thought well, I might as well forget this girl. Well, I was wrong; she was very persistent and wanted to go out one night. I knew this was wrong, but at this point I was not "Mr. Moral."

In fact, everything I did was wrong and immoral. We started a serious affair and it was intense to say the least.

I talked her into getting into this business with me for one reason, no two, she had money and we were dating. So we met with the buyer for the floral department of this big chain store and we were in. They tested us in five stores and within two weeks they approved us for all sixty stores throughout Dallas – Fort Worth. Man, what a trip! Look what I had done. This was amazing. Look at me, look at me, that's the way I was, very arrogant and cocky on the outside and the most insecure, self-centered, jealous man on the planet on the inside.

We were on our way and making some money for a little while. Julie had to put everything in her name and put up all the money. She put all her trust in me; she even quit her job to work there with me. We rented a warehouse in Irving Texas, right next to the Cowboy's stadium. We were pumping out bouquets, and we started to get in over our heads. I called my brother Mike who was back in Houston at this time and asked him if he wanted a job. He did not hesitate so he and his two girls moved up to the Dallas area. Mike was clean at the time and taking care of his girls on his own, and I am sure he thought I was clean too. The fact is I was not using drugs, just drinking. But it was not long after Mike got up there that I ran into a guy at his apartment and had a beer with him and heroin came up, and he knew right where to get it. So once again I was off and running, and in a matter of a few months I racked up ten thousand dollars in hot checks and was hooked on heroin, and I mean hooked bad. I was using every day and a lot of it. This was around the time the famous white Bronco chase was going on, and I remember watching the start of that trial and thinking I am worse off than him. Julie and Mike had left and I was living in the shop taking showers in the sink. I was a mess and strung out worse than ever. The electricity was about to get shut off, I had no car and I was stuck in that shop with nowhere to go and I surely couldn't write any more hot checks. I would have, it's just that no one would take them.

Suicide Attempt

I was watching the trial of the century on TV. And feeling very sick from withdrawal I decided that I couldn't take this anymore. I pulled out a razor blade and started slicing my left wrist. I was cutting so deep my pinky and ring finger were twitching with every cut. I hit a vein that started shooting blood out in a stream; I thought ok, I did it. I laid there bleeding and fell asleep. To my surprise I woke up with the sun beaming through the front windows of the shop and it was the worst feeling in the world. I got up and wrapped an old dirty sock around my wrist and called my drug buddy to come pick me up so I could try to cash a check. We are persistent and I tried enough places and finally got one cashed for three hundred dollars.

It was sometime during the summer in Texas, when it is always hot and I was wearing a sweat jacket to not only hide my needle marks, but the sock of blood I had wrapped around my arm. I checked into a motel and sent him to score me some heroin and cocaine, mostly coke. I had planned that night to do one big shot and explode my heart and die. So he left and headed for Oak Cliff to score and I waited for what seemed like hours. When he returned he had a case of beer and some pot. He said, "Sorry, dude, I couldn't find any boy or girl."(heroin and cocaine)

That was a lie. I never went looking for dope and couldn't find it. So he left and I was there all alone with beer and weed, not my cup of tea at all. But I surely smoked it and drank it.

At this time my brother had gone by the candy shop to check on me and walked in and saw a puddle of blood the size of a good size kitchen table. He was scared to death and thought someone had killed me and dumped me in a dumpster somewhere.

Sometime that night I called him from the hotel and he told me if I call Jim, a guy we had met at meeting, he knew a place in Mabank, Texas, I could go to for treatment. I thought there is no way I am going to treatment. But after sitting in that motel room, check out time approaching, no car, and no money and of course no dope, I was up against a brick wall. I had no choice so I called him.

The Ranch

This is where most definitely the seed of God was sown into my heart. It was a long-term rehab way out in the country miles from any paved road let alone a highway. I walked into the office and this big man was sitting behind a desk and he peered at me over his glasses. "Son, you ready to give God a try?" he asked.

I replied, "Sure, I am dying out there."

"Well, if you give six months of your life I will help you," he said with a serious look.

I thought, well I have nowhere else to go, I didn't say that, just thought it. This is where I first heard, "if you want something you have never had, you must be willing to do something you have never done." Mickey said it all the time. I now always include that quote I had heard so many years ago whenever I tell my story. I spent about two months there and left against the wishes of Mickey and returned to my old life. I was using right away and this is when I started my life of crime and homelessness.

You Have the Right to Remain Silent

I was out of The Ranch for a few months, not going to meetings, not praying, not doing anything to try and stay clean. I had gotten back together with my kids' mom sometime after I got out of The Ranch for the first time. I was working in Dallas for a flower shop and stopped by a sports bar on the way home and drank a beer, then another, and another. Well that was that, I went to Oak Cliff to find Randy, the guy who I used to do heroin with when I had the candy business. It didn't take long and I found him and I was back on heroin and hooked within days.

I hid it from my work, kids, and ex-wife for a while, but it was about to all be revealed. Randy and I were driving very late one night in a bad part of Dallas. We had just scored about eight baskets (a basket is one pill of heroin and one pill of cocaine and a pill is a gel cap filled with the drug). We were on our way out of the neighborhood and there they were red and blue lights. It was three a.m. and I was in a neighborhood that you don't drive through at that time, actually anytime. It was a drug infested area and you were only there for one reason, drugs. We saw the lights and I said, "Eat it!" We both had four baskets. I ate mine and I thought he ate his too.

"Sir, could you step out of the car, what brings you to this side of town?" the officer asked. Make no mistake, he knew.

"We were trying to score but couldn't find any," I replied.

"Let me see your arms," he demanded. I had fresh tracks and many old tracks (tracks are the point of entry where the needle goes in). "Well, you have done a shot recently, I see blood on your arm and sleeve."

"I've got one," his partner said from the driver's side of the car. I thought how in the world had they found something that we ate? His partner brought back one basket he found on the driver's side floor-board and laid it on the trunk. "Sir, you have the right to remain silent…" You get the point.

I was booked into Dallas County Jail on April Fool's day of 1996, for possession of a controlled substance. I really tried to stay clean from that point on and just couldn't. I went to court a few months later and got a two year suspended sentence and five years probation. Let me tell you, this is how powerful addiction can be. I knew if I failed a urinalysis I was going to jail for two years. That was not enough to stop me from going out drinking and eventually losing my job, getting kicked out of my ex-wife's house again, and not seeing my kids. I was hooked again and now on probation.

Drug Motels

I was in Dallas and started staying in drug motels throughout the city. There are many motels around the area that are plagued with drugs and prostitution. I mean 24/7 drugs and girls are out there even as I write this book. I lived in this off and on for years. I would go out and steal beer out of a grocery store, usually ten or so cases and take them around and sell them at construction sites, corners, or even the motel I was staying at. I would get ten dollars per case and keep one to drink, pay for my hotel room and get my drugs. This went on every day for months. I didn't really consider this my homeless state; after all, I was in a place with a bed, shower and a roof. I was sinking further and further into the world of crime that went along with being a street junky. As long as I was able to get high everything was ok. It is so sad to look back on that life today and remember those feelings. It was sick and I didn't even feel like I was that bad off. There is a whole other world out there that many people don't even know exist. That world! These are people just like me, addicts and alcoholics who don't even realize there is a better way of life. I hope and pray that this book is able to get passed on to someone so they can someday see what I see today. Literally there are hundreds of junkies in and out of these hotels at any given time, some old, some kids, moms, dads and even grandparents. They are there and if they are weekend warriors, they don't realize how close they are to being sucked into the life full time.

I remember one time I had stolen some cartons of cigarettes and was trying to sell them with some dude I met in one of these seedy motels. He got out of my car, which by the way was stolen, and he took my cigarettes that I stole! Well, that was not going to fly; I went looking for him around the different motels and found him. He was in a room and I was standing outside my car and screaming, "Get your butt out here you freaking punk!"

He did, and let's just say he wasn't too scared. He came toward me and I had a crowbar behind my back I brought it around and took a swing. I missed! He looked at me and grinned and said, "You just dug your grave, cracker!"

He lunged at me and we fell back in the car and I thought I was dead. Somehow I held on to that crowbar and was able to get it up side his head and he backed up, blood pouring out of his head. He started stumbling over toward a pick up truck, I'm sure to find something to get out and start hitting me with, or a gun. I am not too sure. He had dropped three cartons of my cigarettes on the pavement when he came at me. So needless to say I got them and was very proud of myself and gained some serious street cred. The bad thing was I found out later that night this guy had just got out of prison from doing fifteen flat (that is fifteen straight years).

I did not get much rest that night back in my room; I slept with my crow bar and jumped at every sound I heard. The next night me and another guy were driving around in that stolen car, I never knew who or where the car was stolen from, I just knew I was driving a hot car. We had stolen some beer earlier that afternoon so I had money and was looking for some dope and then a room.

As it turned out we didn't get any heroin but we got some crack and were pulling into a motel to get a room, and once again I saw red and blue lights. This time I had too much to eat so I tried to hide it. They shined a light on the car, had us step out and walk backwards, to the sound of their voice, yes just like on the "Cops" show, and that was that. I was arrested for possession of cocaine and unauthorized use of a motor vehicle. I was in big trouble, and believe it or not I was relieved. It was like, ok, well, it is over; now I will have to quit. It will be in prison but I will be clean and come out clean.

That is a crazy thought, but I do remember those thoughts going through my head. Plus the guy I smashed with the crow bar was looking for me and I had heard when any of them saw the car they were going to start shooting! So going into jail didn't seem all that bad. I was booked into the Dallas County Jail almost one year after the last arrest, only this was a worse charge and I was on probation. After about a week in there I called my dad and told him what was going on and that I was probably not going to get out of this one. He flew from Maryland to come see me and the look on his face was that same look I had seen for years from anyone who loved me: shame, disgust, but there was also some fear in his eyes, he was scared I was going to prison. The sad thing is at this point in my addiction people were happier when I was in jail, at least then they knew I was alive. It is a look I hope I never have to see again from anyone for the rest of my life.

I sat in jail for about three weeks and a miracle happened. I was called out of my cell and taken to a room and told I was being released. The court appointed attorney told me the car was taken from someone who had rented it from a car rental place and they did not want to pursue charges so that meant no car charge, and with no car charge the cocaine couldn't be pinned on me. I didn't really understand that but I didn't care. I was free and walked out of jail.

The Ranch (Round Two)

This was a big turning point for me. It is the first time I made a smart decision. I had a choice go back to the motels or call Mickey. I chose Mickey and called him and he let me back in. I stayed there for over a year this time and was on my way to a glorious Christian walk. When I got back to the ranch I was in trouble with probation. I had Mickey call the probation office and it was all worked out. All I had to do was complete the program and I would be out in good standing with probation.

Well, that turned out to be a tough task. Mickey was very hard on me this time around. I remember one time I had been there for around three months and was about to go on a pass to see my kids. Literally the day they were to pick me up to go and see them, he called me into his office and said, "Son, I am not going to let you go on this pass."

I remember thinking how can you do this, my kids were on their way. I just said, "Ok Mickey, amen," and I went back to my room and probably flipped out. But I knew to not let Mickey see this, because a lot of times it was a test to see how you would react. He told me later that he wanted me to see what it would be like to be in prison and not see my kids at all. He was always doing things that seemed crazy. For example, waking us up at two in the morning to have a complete room and dorm change. This was a lesson in dealing with unmet expectations.

Another time he had me in charge of a group of guys planting bushes in front of the main house. Well, I had been up most of the night with a newcomer to the house. So after planting the bushes I laid down for a nap. All of a sudden I heard this screaming from the yard. "Tim Weber, get out here! You call this a good job, look at the line of bushes, one of them is out of place!" he bellowed.

I kid you not, there was one bush an inch off from the rest of them. "Dig them all up and re-plant 'em," he said.

"Are you freaking kidding me, what is your problem with me, Mickey?" I screamed. "I am not doing it, I will leave before I dig those up," I said, knowing for sure I would go straight to jail if I left rehab.

Needless to say I calmed down and was out digging till late that night. At the time I really thought Mickey hated me, but I grew to understand that he loved me and all of us at the ranch. He was really teaching us so much about acceptance, patience, and how to deal with unmet expectations. Mickey is an ex-pro football player and dynamic speaker. I won't tell his story, but he has been there and God has called him to save the sick. By the sick I mean young men with addictions and in my opinion there is no other place around like the ranch. I will always be forever indebted to him for the God he introduced me to, my Lord and Savior Jesus Christ.

When my time was up at the ranch I was sent to another place for another six months. It was sort of a halfway house with very strict rules and another place where the

Word of God and a twelve-step program are the focus. I really did well there; I completed the program and moved out into a little apartment in Dallas, got a job at a flower shop in the area and thought I had made it. I was going to a few twelve-step meetings a week, but not getting involved in the program. I had no sponsor, I wasn't working the steps and I had stopped going to church and even praying. All I did was work, stop by a meeting late, then leave early, come home and maybe see my kids on the weekend.

It was not long before I picked up a drink, and soon after I started smoking crack. At first, like always I was hiding it from work, girlfriends and my kids. But the disease of addiction is very progressive even when we are not using. Sounds strange, but it is most definitely true. Within a month I had lost my job and was back on heroin and in that same boat. About a week after losing my job, my car was repossessed and my phone was ringing off the wall. I was back in debt; strung out, had no car and I'd disappointed my kids once again. I can't explain how bad that feels when you know you have just screwed everything and everyone around you yet again.

At this point I had no choice but to call my dad and beg for a plane ticket to come back to Maryland. Well, like always he had me a ticket and I was on a plane that day and headed for Baltimore.

The Dating Service

Within one day of being back in Columbia, Maryland, I got a job with my brother Pat at a dating service where he was working. I was a telemarketer and we called people who requested a call for information about our service. It was a really easy job and I worked for my brother, who was the boss of the center. So once again I had it easy, I had a car given to me by my father and was making some money and all was well in Tim's world, for a minute. My friend Toby was here in Maryland and we hooked up again and were both actually going to meetings together and trying to stay sober.

Well, Mary and I met up again and I was back in her and Polly's life again. It wasn't long before I was living with Mary at her farm in Maryland. I was working at the dating service and living with Mary and I started using again. Not much at first, just a few vicodin with a girl I worked with. But anyone who knows the disease of addiction would have known I was about to head right back to heroin. And I did very soon. I had gotten a promotion at the dating service and was now a sales rep, which meant I met with people and tried to sell them a service. It cost anywhere from one thousand dollars to three thousand dollars. I was always shocked when I would make a sale. After all, these people were paying all this money for a chance to meet their soul mate. It really did work for some of them and they would even send in letters letting us know that they were getting married.

Code Blue Overdose

I was working out in Fairfax, Virginia, one day and I was using, I was shooting heroin and cocaine (speedballs). I had done one before I got to work and after I was there I hid a syringe in the office. I was with a client and had just made a big sale, so I grabbed my syringe and went to the bathroom. I pulled the syringe out of my sock and sat on the toilet. I stuck the needle in my arm, shot the dope and stuck the syringe back in my sock and walked out and went to the gift shop in the office building. My office was in a big office building along with a lot of other businesses. As I walked into the gift shop, I remember putting some Starburst on the counter and then I started shaking and that is all I remember until waking up in an ambulance.

"Tim, Tim can you hear me?" the paramedic was asking me. "We know your history," he said, meaning they knew I was a heroin addict. One of the girls at the office had told them. They had shot me full of Narcon, a drug to reverse the affects of heroin. I was taken to the hospital and released a few hours later. Mary had come to pick me up and we went home to her house. I had another pill of heroin and the syringe still on me and pulled it out at home and told Mary, "That's it, I am done." I flushed it down the toilet and thought, I almost died, I will never do this again.

It amazes me to this day how they didn't find that syringe and pill of dope. I found out the next day that I was blue, foaming at the mouth and not breathing; I was dead in the courtyard! My friend at work called me and told me all this the next day. I remember her saying, "Dude, did you see God? Cause you were dead, Tim."

Well, I didn't see God but I really thought that was going to be it. I really wanted to quit doing heroin and get straight, but the very next day when that heroin withdrawal kicked in later that morning I was on my way to Baltimore. I went to one of my corners, found two pills of heroin and two pills of coke and went to an abandoned house with some other addicts and got high for the next three days. At the time I was stealing disposable cameras from different superstores and selling them at bars in Baltimore, then using the money to get high. I would do this all day, then at some point during the night I would lay down on some old newspapers and try and sleep until that insistent urge from the heroin would wake me up and I was off to do it another day.

This is when I started my long stretches of homelessness. Mary finally had enough and we went our separate ways and I don't blame her at all for that. I know all she ever wanted was for me to be clean and sober either with her or without her.

The Bottom Starts

I was living in an abandoned row house on Washington Boulevard, in Baltimore. This is where I lived on and off for the last year of my addiction and let me tell you it was hell on earth. The place had no electricity, no running water, no toilet; it was nasty. There would be people in the house at all times, some upstairs shooting dope, some at the kitchen table smoking crack. Prostitutes doing their thing in different rooms, usually getting just enough money to do a shot of dope, and then hit the street to find another "John" to get money from. We ripped people off that would come to the city looking for dope. I had become a street rat just looking for any way I could to get ten dollars. I did a lot of "boosting," that is stealing stuff from stores and then either returning it to the same store I stole it from or selling it to someone at a hole in the wall bar in the city. I did this every day.

At one point I ran into a guy who had some fake money. Kind of monopoly type money only better, and late at night you could rip off dope dealers on the streets. I had stolen a lot of this money from the guy who had it so I was on a run for a while with this scam. I got really stupid and I even started doing it during the day. This was very dangerous and I had bricks thrown through my car window, knives thrown at me, and guns drawn on me many times for this craziness. Yet I would stay in the same ten-mile radius, because that is where I knew my dope was and that is where I laid my head every day. I woke up every day and wanted to die, every day! It was hell but I just did not know how to stop.

I was getting further and further into this street lifestyle. It is sad but the people I ran the streets with were just like me. They are lost and just need to open their hearts, let God in and try recovery. They are there right now, hoping someone will save them but just not knowing who that is. Wishing they could change, wishing they could live life, and not just exist. I know it as sure as I am sitting here writing this story. I can't explain the emptiness you feel when you pull yourself up off a floor in an abandoned house and walk the streets looking for a cigarette butt to try and get at least two hits off of. Then figuring out how to get ten dollars to get your first shot of the day, all the while the Ravens are playing, the sun is shining, people are walking to the stadium, smiling, laughing and wearing their jerseys, and living life. It feels like crap so you find your ten dollars, do your shot and hope it is of good quality so you can attempt to hide these emotions and move forward through the rest of that day.

I over dosed two more times during this period. Once I was driving my car, pulled over and did a shot of heroin, stuck the needle in the trunk, pulled out of the gas station, got to a light under 95 and Washington Boulevard and just blacked out. I stopped breathing. I woke up to paramedics, the police, and a fire truck. They were shaking me and asked me what I had taken. They had shot me full of Narcon so they knew it was heroin or some kind of opiate. I refused treatment and, I kid you not, they let me just pull my car over to the side and wait a while and then I could leave.

This was one of the times I somehow had a car so one of the ways I would get money was by "hacking." Hacking is picking up people in the city who need a ride, it could be anyone from a little old lady going to church to a dope dealer going from the east side of Baltimore to the west side. Either way it was five, ten, or twenty dollars. And sometimes when it was a dealer you get to cut out the money and get the dope right then and there. This just so happened to be who I got the dope from the day I over dosed under that bridge. That is the thing with buying heroin, you never know how pure it is, and you are playing Russian roulette every time you stick that needle in your arm. I left from that situation under the 95 bridge and never stopped. I was on a path that would eventually lead to the point of sure death if I were to keep going.

Why Toby and Not Me?

May of 2001 I got news my dear friend Toby had died. I was at someone's apartment getting high. I was wanted by the police for a few charges stemming from assault to a hit and run of a parked vehicle. Mary called me and said, "Toby is dead." It hit me right between the eyes and it hurt badly. Not only was he dead, but he and I had a falling out a few months back and hadn't talked in a while. Honestly, Toby was tired of me and concerned about my life and like a lot of people he was worried I was going to end up dead.

He also was good friends with Mary and was put in a position of loving me as a friend and her as well. And let's just say I was a complete jerk to Mary. I did some horrible things to Mary from stealing stuff from her to cheating on her while she was out of town once. And Toby knew a lot of this stuff and had told her. In his defense the only reason it came out was because I was missing one time in Mary's car and they were looking for me.

Anyway, when I got the news I freaked out! I was staying with a girl I was using with and I was in and out of her house all the time. Well, the day of Toby's funeral I was getting dressed and there was a knock at the door. My girlfriend went to the door and said, "Who is it?"

They replied, "Howard County Sheriff's Department, Warrant Squad, we are looking for Timothy Dale Weber."

"He is not here," she said.

I was in the bedroom and heard it all. I ran through the back door in my boxers and dress socks and made it out across the back of the apartments to my car, which I had parked two complexes over just for this situation. Well, needless to say they were not leaving; I kept calling from a pay phone and asking if they were gone.

"No, they are parked out front," she told me.

Finally, I called Mary and told her and she let me come out to her house. So I missed the viewing, funeral and everything because I was afraid they would go there looking for me. I still regret that to this day. I often wondered back then, how could Toby die? He had everything going for him. He was not nearly as bad off with drugs as me and he was, bright, good-looking, and could do anything. Why him and not me?

I stayed at Mary's to hide out basically. I was a mess. I was sick from not having any dope and didn't stay long, maybe a day or so and then I took off and was back in the city getting high.

I somehow ended up living in Pennsylvania with the girl I drank and got high with. She had moved there and was more than willing to let me stay with her. We had a very sick relationship, and we fed off each other's disease so much. I really cleaned up a little bit while I was in Pennsylvania. At least I was only drinking for a while. But as I said earlier if you are an addict you can only quiet the storm for a while. It is always brewing up in you ready to explode. It was just too crazy there and if

I am being honest, I probably wanted to use heroin and didn't even know it, and I sure didn't know where to score there. So I left.

I don't know where she is today, but I do pray she has found recovery somewhere. I stayed with her only two or three weeks and decided I wanted to come back to Maryland. I didn't even tell her I was leaving I just sneaked out of her house early one morning and left, leaving half my clothes there.

My Guardian Angel

I called my dad and asked him to pick me up halfway between Pennsylvania and Maryland. And of course he did. I am sure I told him I was clean, and technically I was. When I got home he said my brother Mike was there and needed help moving his old girlfriend's stuff out of his basement. Well, I was in no mood for this, but I had no choice. I was at their mercy. After all, I knew I had to play the game to get what I wanted. I was back at Dad's with no job, no car and no plans.

I told my brother that I would help with one load and that's it. But that all changed because my brother's ex was bringing a friend to help. Well, when I saw her my heart dropped. She was tall, brown hair, brown eyes, and the most incredible smile. She also had the shape and curves of a supermodel. My attitude quickly changed and I was willing to move as many loads as needed. Her name was Kathy and she is most definitely my guardian angel. We spent that day moving and then went our separate ways.

I was trying at this time to stay clean and I was even going to meetings in Columbia. I knew if my brother's ex had anything to do with it, this girl wouldn't give me a second thought. She had told her, "He is trouble, big trouble. You don't want to have anything to do with him."

Well, a few days later they asked to take Mike and I to lunch for our efforts in the move. I jumped at this opportunity and went. I had started a job at an equipment rental place in Catonsville, Maryland, so I was looking like I was trying and I am very lovable when I am clean and sober (at least I think so). It was that day that I found out that she had been thinking of me as much as I was thinking of her.

Now Kathy was a college graduate and working for a major accounting firm, and I was a drug addict making nine dollars an hour renting a room somewhere. Not the best catch in the world you might say. We ended up going out on a date to see the Baltimore Orioles play, and we talked the whole game and didn't even see one at bat. It was soon after, maybe two weeks, when I disappeared and went to the city and started using heroin again. I had told her at one point very early on that I am subject to disappear at any given moment. And sure enough, I did. I disappeared for about three days. When I returned to my room that I was renting from a guy, no one was home so I just went in like nothing was wrong. But I was soon woken up by my dad, the police, and my roommate, and I was asked to leave. My dad took his keys to the car he had let me use, the guy took his keys to the house, and there I was with nowhere to go. So I called Kathy and she picked me up and drove me around for hours. We ended up at a motel and I still don't know where that was. I was really coming off heroin badly and I was sweating so badly that night I covered the sheets with my perspiration. Kathy stayed in the other bed and said she watched me all night and I would jump, shake and moan, all night.

The next morning she said she had to take me somewhere and it wasn't going to be her house. So I chose Howard

County General Hospital. I knew I could go in there and tell them I was suicidal and they would have to keep me for seventy–two hours. This is a trick all a hard core addicts have used at some point in their addiction. I got to Howard County General and went in and said I was going to kill myself and they took me back and I said good bye to Kathy. That was a very bad feeling, I really figured it would be the last time I would see her.

I got through my seventy-two hours and was released. My dad picked me up and I was out and in another room for rent right away. I got another car from my dad and was seeing Kathy again and really giving recovery a try. (Well… as much as someone who has not been allowed to hit bottom can be trying.)

I want to take a minute to say this. My dad, God love him, wanted nothing more than for me to have a happy life. He tried so hard to do whatever he thought was right to help me, but he could never truly help me until he took the advice of others and let me fall. That means doing whatever it took to not enable me. I know this was hard on him and he had many sleepless nights wondering if his youngest son was dead or alive. Being a father myself I can empathize with him today. I would probably make the same mistakes he did with the enabling. But I do know this, the only way to love an addict and help them is to let them fall, and fall hard. I am not saying don't help at all but under no circumstances bail them out for years, like my dad did.

OK, back to the addict. I was working at a candy vending service place and seeing Kathy. As long as I was clean Kathy would see me, and when I would get off track she would distance herself from me. She loved me from afar, and prayed her heart off!

The stay at Howard County General didn't last long and I was using soon after I was released. It was around this time my girlfriend and her family were heading out on a vacation to St Barth's. I was asked to stay at Kathy and her brother's house and watch the cat and the house. Remember, at this time everyone thought I was clean. But in reality I had started dabbling again in my drugs, not quite hooked with a bad habit yet, but well on my way. This was in July of 2003 and it would be five more months of hell before I allowed God to intervene and my life was saved. I had Kathy's Jeep and as soon as she left and got on the plane I was in Baltimore and did not stop for weeks. She came back I think seven days later and I was to pick her up at the airport and I was no where to be found. During her trip we did talk on the phone and I of course acted like everything was fine. This again shows how powerful this drug addiction can be. I knew she was coming home that day. I got up at her brother's house sicker than a dog, by now I was hooked again after seven straight days of shooting speed balls. I even stole her brother's change and a lot of his DVD's, to get high. I really hope all this is hitting someone hard, because this is the truth about addiction. It turns normal, good people into monsters, and animals who will do anything to anyone at anytime in order to feed their addiction. I knew full well that they would know I took this stuff, and I didn't care – well, I did, but my disease didn't.

I hurt, and embarrassed Kathy so much not showing up at the airport to pick her up. Her whole family was there, and I didn't show. Then she got home with her brother and the house looked like they had been robbed, and in essence they were. Not only that, I had her car and I stayed gone for another few days after she was gone.

I was in Baltimore and she had not heard from me yet so she came looking for me, and she found me. I saw her pull up and I had just done a shot of dope five minutes earlier and when I saw her I thought I was going to pass out. She pulled up to me looked me in the eyes and said the most loving thing someone could have ever said to me. "Tim, you are a good man, and you deserve better," she said with the saddest look in her eyes.

I told her where her jeep was and she drove off. A couple of days later I had another overdose on Washington Boulevard. I had done a shot and walked out of the abandoned house I was visiting and I blacked out. Again I woke up to police and paramedics, they shot me full of Narcon and, when I woke up, I looked into the street and standing in the middle of the street was Kathy. As plain as day I saw her looking at me. I even told the paramedics my girlfriend is going to drive me home. They asked "Where is she?" and I pointed to the street. They said there was no one there. I looked again and she was gone. I went to a pay phone and called her and she said she was not there at all. I know in my heart she was watching over me in spirit and prayer.

It was a few days later. I went back to my room and Kathy came by to check on me. Meanwhile, my dad was obtaining a court order to have me picked up on a protective custody order, which is when you are a danger to your self or others. And I was, I wanted to die, and I could have killed someone anytime I drove. Sometime later that day I was picked up by the police and taken to Howard County General Hospital on a court order. When you are taken into the hospital for a court order they take your clothes and put you in a hospital gown. After a few hours I was tired of waiting on a doctor to come evaluate me, and not feeling too good from not having any dope. I was well on the verge of getting dope sick soon. So I ran out the Emergency Room door in my gown, no underwear and no shoes. I made it maybe a block and the police had been called and it was that quick, I was handcuffed and brought back to the hospital and a guard posted outside my room door.

The doctor came in, a psychiatrist, who I had seen many times before from when I would voluntarily come in to eat and clean up for three days. He said, "I have no choice but to commit you, Tim, you're going to be sent to Springfield Hospital." This is a lockdown facility in Sykesville, Maryland. I got there around three in the morning and slept till around ten the next morning. When I woke up I was in a place where there were really crazy people, not drug addicts, crazy people. Looking back I was just as crazy as the ones in there who were seeing and hearing things and thought they were turning into a lizard. Yes, one guy was turning into a lizard and you couldn't tell him any different. But how crazy was I? I kept doing the same thing over and over again expecting different results. I was probably thirty-six years old at this time and I knew every time I took a drink of alcohol I would end up using drugs, going to jail, becoming homeless and losing everything, yet I continued to do it. So who was crazier, me or the lizard man?

Well, to show you again the depths we will go in order to continue using drugs and fight recovery listen to this craziness. I noticed it took three seconds for the door to close after someone walked through it, so I watched a nurse walk through and I made my way to the door and put my foot in the door. I looked behind me, no one saw me, so out the door I went. When you got to this hospital you were able to get dressed in your street clothes, so I was now in the corridor and needed to get out of another locked door. Addicts are very intuitive and I knew I could get out. I walked the long hallway, found a nurse on the other end and said, "Hi, I was here visiting my brother and I got locked in, could you please let me out."

She answered, "Sure, sir" and opened the door and I was free. So now I was out of the locked area I still had to figure out where the heck I was. I walked into the security office and right up to an officer. "Sir, I was up here visiting my brother and my car won't start, could you give me a ride up to the Highs store?" I had heard people talking about a Highs convenience store up the road during my short stay.

He said, "Sure, buddy, no problem."

OK, so now I was completely off the grounds, now I just had to get home, with no money and no car. I asked someone who was walking into the store if he could give me a ride to Howard County. I have no idea why but he did. And there I was, home, probably twenty-four hours after being picked up by the police and escaped from two places and now I was in my bed. All was well in Tim's world.

I called Kathy, gave her some crazy story, I think I told her they let me out early to go to a rehab or something, so I asked her to stop by. I didn't know, but the hospital called her soon after and said I had escaped, and she told them I was home. So the same police who originally picked me up were back at my house and returned me to Springfield, where I spent two weeks.

This is where the end was nearing. I had two doctors there who would not let me get away with anything; they were great. I didn't think so then but looking back I know they played a huge part in my recovery. I still stop by Springfield to this day and let them know I am doing well and what I am up to.

Part Two

What Happened to Change Me

The Look that Changed My Life

OK, every addict must hit bottom; here is mine. I had been in a halfway house in Baltimore and had about thirty days clean and sober, Kathy was happy, my family was happy and I thought I was on my way this time. I was going to meetings and doing the right thing; I had a job and was really trying. Well, this is another example of how powerful and insidious this disease is. I was out on my pass and Kathy and I went to visit a friend of hers. Her boyfriend was an active addict, and I was thirty days clean and sober, and Kathy was so proud of me. The girl's boyfriend asked me to give him a ride to the store. But he was up to no good and actually went into the store to steal something. He came out and then asked me to give him a ride to sell it in the city. I can't believe I did this, I had no plans in using but he went into a house and I knew he was in there shooting coke. After about ten minutes I went in and could not resist and I had a needle in my arm in minutes. I did not go back to the girl's house and pick up Kathy and she had to find a ride home. Understand this, this girl did not use drugs and Kathy surely had nothing to do with drugs. They were just both caught in the middle of two disgusting addicts. Kathy found out later her friend had lied to her about her boyfriend. She told Kathy he had been clean and sober for close to a year, so Kathy thought he would be a good person for me to be around.

I finally came back to the house and Kathy was back over there and she was waiting on me. And she was furious! She yelled, screamed and really let me have it. We ended up leaving together and the next day she gave me a ride back out to their house to pick up my dad's truck. We had talked all night and I was supposed to go into a long-term rehab the next day.

The next day I still had money in my pocket and when she dropped me off I had something else in mind. We headed out, her in her jeep in front of me, and me in my dad's truck. When we got to the road where I should have gone in one direction to head to the rehab, I didn't. I went toward Baltimore. She saw this and she gave me a look that saved my life. A look of shame, disgust, fear, and how could you do this to me, your kids, and everyone who loves you? It was a look like you have heard throughout this book that I had grown accustomed to. However, this time it hit me like a ton of bricks. This was the first time in my life that God allowed me to feel, I mean really feel some emotions. They were intense and I saw that same look I had given to all the people who loved me all the way to Baltimore.

It was the same look my son gave me one day when he was four or five and had a basketball in his hand and wanted me to shoot some hoops with him. He said, "Dad, please don't go!" I told him I would be back soon. And he replied, "No you won't, you never come back when you leave." And he was right.

I also thought of another time I was supposed to take my kids and nieces to Six Flags and I left on a Friday and never came home until Monday. My brother had come and picked his kids up and when I walked in the house my little blonde haired daughter Megan was at the door and she gave me that look of shame, disgust, what have I done to deserve a father like you! She was probably twelve at the time and she was mad and hated me for years for that. There were so many broken promises, not just that one particular event. Another time my grandmother died and I took all our money and was behind the Cotton Bowl in Dallas shooting dope through the whole funeral. I finally emerged days later and saw that same look on everyone's face. In every one of these situations, drugs were more important to me than anything.

I thought about all that stuff all the way to the city. And I know this was my intervention from God, because up until this point I was as cold as ice. I did not feel anything, I might have acted like it at times but I didn't. I could make a tear show up in the corner of my eye at the right time when needed to get what I wanted, but this was different. I was all alone, just me and God in that car, and it hurt and it hurt bad. I did have money so I continued to the city and I got high. But it did not work, I was high; however, I could not get those feelings out of my head. This was sometime around November 6th, 2003.

November 8th, 2003

On November 8th , 2003 I walked into Howard County General Hospital and said I was going to kill myself once again. They took me back and I saw one of the same doctors I had seen forever doing this bit. She looked at me and said, "Tim, you are not going to kill yourself, you are an addict and an alcoholic and we can't help you here anymore."

Well, I looked at her with the most desperate and serious look I have ever had. "PLEASE, PLEASE. I AM BEGGING YOU," I screamed.

"You are right. I am probably not going to kill myself, but I am dying out there and if you don't help me I will die, or end up in prison for the rest of my life."

Again, God stepped in and had to have touched that doctor, because she did a complete 180, and said, "OK, Tim, but if you miss one group, go late to dinner, smoke in the bathroom or do one thing out of line I will have you kicked out."

So I entered the hospital and from that day forward my life has changed 100%. I did everything in there that I was supposed to do, I was at group on time, cleaned up other people's trays after dinner, I mean I was the perfect resident. I called the halfway house I was in a month earlier and they said I could come back. I left Howard County General Hospital and entered the halfway house with a new attitude; I was at that point where every addict must be, wanting recovery and not just needing it. It was a run-down row house on Linwood Avenue in Baltimore, not five blocks from where I used to score dope. The thing is it doesn't matter where you are when you are ready to receive God and recovery. It is an inside job. I linked up with a group of guys at the house who were serious about God and recovery. I got a sponsor in my twelve-step group and I started to work the steps toward recovery. It was very hard, for the first time I was exposed to every feeling and emotion in the world. I drove Kathy crazy with all my insecurities and jealousies. I knew I had all this but I was able to keep it at bay with the drugs and alcohol. Now it was gone. I would ask her everywhere we went, "Do you want that guy, why were you looking at him, why this, why that?" I was crazy. And I never thought I could let everybody know I was that way. But trust me, there are a lot of people out there that way, especially addicts. We feel so bad about ourselves we don't know what to do.

Thankfully, I can tell you now what I did, I stayed sober and worked through the twelve steps and became a productive member of society. I got a job and started catching a bus in Baltimore to work. I made six dollars an hour pulling staples at some kind of insurance records place. I literally made enough money to catch a bus for a week, pay my hundred dollars a week rent and maybe a hamburger at a fast food place. But I was doing it all on my own and I was feeling really good about that. After a few months there I got another job at a flower shop in the city. I made nine dollars an hour and was able to eventually get a car through the help of my father and my house manager who was selling the car. I was really feeling good. I was praying every day, going to meetings and working. Kathy was coming around with a little trust building and my family was as well. I had made a commitment to stay in the halfway house for six months and then discuss leaving with my sponsor.

Part Three

What it is like today

Cattails Country Florist

Sometime around April of 2004 Kathy and I were taking a friend of mine to a meeting. When we dropped him off, his dad came out and gave me a newspaper clipping of a flower shop for sale in Woodbine, Maryland. I had told him on a number of occasions that I would like to own a flower shop again one day when the time is right. Well, who knew the time would be when I was living in a recovery house with only six months clean and sober! But again God will bless you wherever you are and only He knows when the time is right. So Kathy said, "Call the number. You know you want to."

I replied, "Kathy, they probably want way too much money. And let's not forget I live in a halfway house and make nine dollars an hour."

Well, let me just say this: all things are possible with God on your side. So I called and they wanted a reasonable amount of money for it. Now understand if they wanted two hundred dollars for it that was about one hundred and ninety eight short of what I had. But again, all things are possible. At this time Kathy was working in Virginia for an accounting firm making a lot more money than nine dollars an hour. So the thought of us buying a flower shop together seemed a little bit crazy - that is to everyone but us. We had figured out a way to buy the shop the week of Mother's Day and pay for it with the money we made that week. I knew that if they really did the sales they had shown us this was possible.

We took over the shop on May 1st, 2004 and did exactly what we had planned. The shop was paid off after that first week. We moved to Sykesville, Maryland around the time we bought the shop, ironically right across the street from Springfield Hospital. Now we still had to have extra money to operate and live and it just kept coming in, and God provided everything we needed.

The first year was very tough; we slept on the floor many times and had many sleepless nights. We started slowly growing and we both kept God first and I kept my recovery my number one priority. So here we are, me six months sober, Kathy leaving a job that she had a degree for, and I know she was scared but she did have faith. As for me there was nowhere to go but up, as for her she could leave a job that had all the benefits and pay big companies offer, and possibly lose it all.. But it was working and time rolled on and my first year (clean & sober) anniversary was here November 8th, 2004. I had been planning this event since the first day I got sober, and this time I had invited everyone I knew to my first year anniversary and it was wonderful. All my family, Kathy's family and all my friends in and out of meetings were there. I had planned this speech for a whole year, but I said nothing like I planned.

Will You Marry Me, Again?

After my anniversary, I had planned to propose to Kathy. So this would be the second time I had proposed, the first time was right before she went to Saint Barth's and it was not a good situation. She did say yes, but there was never a date set. In fact, she called it off soon after she returned from St Barth's, and I am sure you can understand why. She had told me she would not even consider marrying me unless I was a year clean and sober. So it was a year that night, and I was ready to ask her again under much better circumstances. I ordered three hundred and sixty five red roses and took them to our apartment and spread them all over the living room and bedroom. There was one rose for every day I was clean and sober. We came home from my celebration and when we got to the house Kathy opened the door and said, "Oh my God, what happened in here?"

If you didn't know what you were looking at, that many roses looked like someone had ransacked our house. After she realized they were roses she went to the bedroom and on her pillow was one white rose with the ring tied to it. She picked it up and I got on my knee and asked, "Will you marry me?"

She replied, "Yes." Then she asked, "What is the white rose for?"

I told her that it is to signify the ring is no longer tainted, and was pure and my motives were pure. So we started planning our wedding for August 21, 2005.

Well, we had our first year at the shop come and go and we were really growing and it was becoming impossible for us to keep up with all our business. Thanks in part to my good friends at The Funeral Home, Jim and Todd, we started a deal on linking our websites and we just exploded with funeral business. This is when we met Mandy, our head designer and Manager, she walked in looking for a job and was hired soon after. She has been such a blessing and is the best designer and friend in the world. This freed me up to deliver and market our business and for Kathy to learn more hands on stuff at the shop. Things just kept getting better at the shop and we eventually hired a full time driver so I could help Mandy with designing. Kathy was turning into quite the astute florist, she is the best wedding consultant around, in my opinion. It is hard to say no to her and her infectious, happy go lucky personality.

The wedding was upon us and let me tell you we were excited. My son was best-man and my daughter was my best lady. Kathy's brother was her "Man of Honor" or as I called him, her "Dude of Honor." Everyone was there and it was a wonderful day I will never forget and will cherish forever. My son's toast to Kathy left not one dry eye in the room:

Guardian Angel

God works in mysterious ways.

You are here and I am glad you are here to stay.

Your spirit soars like a dove.

When I see you and Dad, I know that it's true love.

You make my dad happy and I can see.

You are the best that can be.

When I see ya'll I know it's faith.

I can tell by the smile you put on my dad's face.

You got my dad out of twists and tangles;

You are truly my dad's Guardian Angel.

Michael Dale Weber

8-21-2005

My Brother-in-law's and Father–in-law's toasts just topped the night off. It was one of the best nights of my life to this day. We went to the Bahamas for our honeymoon and it was amazing. I was thinking less than two years ago I was a homeless drug addict, and here I am today on the beach in the Bahamas. How cool is that? God is great!

Super Bowl XLI

The Super Bowl I will never forget and I never saw one down. This was the day my daughter woke up from her coma after having an emergency liver transplant. Five months earlier she had given birth to my grandson Nicholas. She was driving home from work one day and swerved to miss a deer and flipped her car. After one month of being laid up with a broken back she went into liver failure from the pain medication, both over the counter and prescribed. When I got to the hospital she was given 72 hours to live. I was in shock! I tried to hold it together but I must admit I lost it a few times. I did not ever use drugs or drink during this period, but I surely acted like the old Tim a time or two. To make matters worse Megan and I were not speaking at the time and I had not talked to her in over a month. This was a mistake on both our parts; we are both hard headed and headstrong. And we were not giving in. When I walked into Johns Hopkins and saw her, all that fell by the wayside. I just wanted my little girl to live. And it was not looking good, she was third on the transplant list and the hours were ticking away. I flew my son Michael up from Texas where he was living. He was nineteen at the time, and her best chance for a live donor match. You can take part of a good liver and put it in someone else and both halves will grow and work. We had so many people test to be donors; even the doctors at Johns Hopkins said it was unbelievable how many people tried to support us. And I must say a good majority of them were from my recovery meetings, recovering addicts and alcoholics when in recovery are some of the most caring and loving human beings in the world.

As it turned out, no one was a perfect match, except Michael. So the doctor went over the procedure, and he signed all the paperwork and the plan was to have them in surgery the next morning. He was so brave and really wanted to help his sister. I on the other hand was not so brave; I was really scared to lose both of them. I prayed, Kathy prayed, Kathy's mom prayed; let's just say everyone from here to Texas was praying their hearts out. The next morning Michael had an IV in his arm and we were getting ready to walk him down to the Operating Room. But then the doctor walked in and said, "Mr. Weber, we found a liver, it is in Puerto Rico and I am getting on a plane in a half hour to go get it."

We were so relieved, our prayers were answered. Now let me say this, the doctors at Johns Hopkins were fabulous, they never once gave us false expectations, yet always made us comfortable. I mean, who would ever think the head of the liver department at the hospital would actually fly all that way and check the liver out, bring it back, and assist in putting the liver in Megan. Talk about going above and beyond the call of duty. I know they would probably do this for anyone, but they sure made us feel special and we had all the confidence in the world in them.

Well, the liver went in on February 2nd, 2007, and on February 4th, Super Bowl Sunday, I was standing next to Megan as she lay there on a ventilator to breathe for her. There was a small twitch in her hand. You have to understand for close to a week there was nothing, no sign of life at all, so this gave us some needed hope. Then a few hours later I was back in there next to her and all of a sudden her eyes opened. I screamed, "OH MY GOD! SHE IS AWAKE!" I ran down the hallway to the waiting room and yelled, "She is up, my God, she is awake!"

From that point on it was up and down, she slowly started talking through her ventilator and the first words she mouthed to me were, "Dad, I am sorry and I love you."

I thought I was going to die right there, it killed me that we had let things go on for so long. I made a promise right then and there to never let petty things come between me and the people I love. You never know what can happen from one day to the next. We spent close to a year in and out of the hospital and we had many trying days, but God was with us and we made it. I am happy to say Megan is doing great and going to school to be a medical assistant, and is taking care of her son Nicholas.

God, Meetings, Service and Family

Today I am clean and sober and go to at least three meetings a week, I pray everyday, I have a sponsor, I have a home group and I am active in helping others who are lost in this disease of addiction. I volunteer with different groups throughout my community and try to get this message out to anyone who will listen. I was recently appointed to be on the Carroll County Behavior Health & Addiction Planning Committee. I have also gone through a program called Choices to become an instructor for kids who have minor violations with the law ranging from alcohol citations to misdemeanor drug charges. Most recently I have taken a position as The Maryland Director of In the Blink of an Eye Ministries, a non-profit organization to help addicts and families of addicts in there quest for recovery. I have met some of the best people in the world on my journey in recovery. My life is filled with such peace and serenity today. I am so grateful for every breath I take. I was so lost for so long; I now try to take advantage of every second of every day.

I hope that this gives you a little insight into what a drug addict goes through and what they put everyone else through. We are not bad people; we are sick and like any other sickness you must be treated for it. I have found, for me the only treatment that works is a relationship with God and the twelve-step recovery program I am involved with. Because of this treatment I am now one of those people walking to the football game in a Raven's jersey. I am a good father, son, husband, brother, friend and, oh yeah, a grandfather today. I am a respected member of my community and have friends from the States Attorney's office, Maryland State Police, Local Police, Churches and more. I have a life today beyond my wildest dreams, and I will never forget where I came from. So when I see someone homeless on the street, I pray that they meet the God I met and be led out of their despair. I know everyone knows someone who needs to hear a message of hope and hear that there is a way out just like I heard many years ago.

It took a long time for me to move out of the way and let God take over, but now that I have, all things are possible. My wife and I own and operate a very successful flower shop; we own a home and we live just few houses down from my wife's parents and they have become two of our best friends. We do so many fun things together like paintball games, scuba diving, hiking and just hanging out watching football games. The father I feared so much is one of my best friends and golf buddies, we try and play golf once a week during the golf season with my two brothers who are both in recovery as well. Let me tell you, out of all that I have today the most important thing to me is the peace I have on a daily basis. I wake up every day without a guilty conscience, and that is worth a million dollars!

Thank you and God bless you!

Acknowledgments

My recovery and this book would not have been possible without all the people who helped me along the way.

- First and foremost I want to thank God for everything.

- My wife Kathy, who is truly my guardian angel and I love you so much babe, Thank you for believing in me . You are truly the most spiritual, loving and caring person I know.

- My two kids Megan and Michael who sadly had to grow up without a father most of their lives. I love you both more than you may ever know. I will always be here for you.

- My Dad and step mom,(Arlene); I hope that all the years of pain I have caused you both will be replaced with years of joy and happiness. I love you both very much. Thank you for never giving up on me.

- My Mom, Miriam, I hope you are looking down on me saying "That's my Timothy Turtle". I really miss you and the years I lost with you.

- My Brothers Pat and Mike who I fought with growing up but look forward to every second we spend together today, especially on the golf course. I love the both of you so much and thank you for all you have done for me through the years.

- My Grandson Nicholas, what a blessing you are. I hope you only know the Paw-Paw you know today, clean and sober.

- My in-laws Mike and Katie, I am so blessed to have married into a family that is so full of love. I will never forget how you two never made me feel less than, even when I was.

- Mike, Karen and Steve, I thank you all for accepting me and forgiving me for the past and giving me a chance to show you I would be good to your little Roo.

- Isaiah, thanks for introducing me to God and all you do for young people in recovery.

- My sponsor, Spence, thank you for being the example to follow on my journey of recovery. You have helped me more than you will ever know.

- The Storches , I love all of you . You were my home away from home.

- Timmy my house manager at the Linwood House, thank you for all your support.

- All my friends of Bill W. Thanks for telling me to "keep coming back." You know who you are!

- Jim C. I value our friendship so much and thank you for introducing me to George from the Choices program; it has opened so many doors.

- George, Tracy and Anne-Marie from Choices, I look forward to every month we spend together.

- Mandy for all the hard work you do to make our business a success.

- My dog Munchkin, The coolest dog in the world "Ry Ruff Ru"

About the Author

Tim Weber resides in Westminster, Maryland with his wife Kathy. Together they own and operate Cattails Country Florist, Inc. in Woodbine, Maryland. He is the father of two children Megan and Michael and has a grandson named Nicholas and another grandchild on the way. He currently resides on the Behavioral Health and Addictions Planning Committee for Carroll County, The Maryland Director of IBE Ministries, Inc. He is very active in the community with helping other addicts live productive and drug free lives, as well as helping to prevent young adults and teens from going down the path of addiction that he did.

For information on help with drug and alcohol addictions please go to www.theweberaddictiongroup.org or email comments and book reviews to timweber65@comcast.net

CPSIA information can be obtained at www.ICGtesting.com
Printed in the USA
BVOW011907190312

285571BV00002B/1/P